MELTDOWN!

by Jill Murphy

WALKER BOOKS
AND SUBSIDIARIES

LONDON • BOSTON • SYDNEY • AUCKLAND

One morning, Mum decided to take Ruby shopping.
"Ruby can be helping Mummy," said Mum.
"HELPING MUMMY!" shouted Ruby,
jumping up and down with glee.

Then Ruby couldn't stop jumping up and down.

"That's enough jumping," said Mum.
"'Nuff jumping," agreed Ruby.

"Come on," said Mum.
"Into the pushchair
and off we go."

"Off we go," said Ruby. "WHEEEEEE!"

At first, Ruby tried her best to be helpful.
Mum chose things and gave them to Ruby
and Ruby put them into the trolley.

Mum handed Ruby a bag of carrots.
"Can you put *these* in the trolley, please?"
asked Mum.

"*In* the trolley!"
said Ruby proudly,
dropping them in.

Then Mum handed Ruby a
big pack of crisps.
"In they go!"
said Mum.

"*In* they go!" said Ruby,
scrunching the pack to
make it crackle.

"Not scrunching things, Ruby," said Mum. "Do it properly."
"Prop'ly," said Ruby.

Mum handed Ruby a loaf of bread.

"Can you put *this* in the trolley, please?" she asked.

"*In* the trolley!" said Ruby, throwing the bread up
in the air.

"Not throwing it!" said Mum. "Do it nicely."

"Nicely," agreed Ruby.

Then Mum handed Ruby a tin of beans.
Ruby bent down and rolled it along the floor.
"Rolling it!" she said. "Rolling along!"

"RIGHT!" said Mum. "If you can't help me
properly, you'd better go in the seat."

"*In* the seat!" said Ruby, grabbing the trolley and running off with it.

"COME BACK HERE, RUBY!" shouted Mum. "You'd better stop right now or there'll be trouble – AND I MEAN IT!"

"You're *not* being very helpful, Ruby," said Mum, plonking her into the trolley.

"Not very helpful," agreed Ruby, sadly.

Mum trundled into the cake section.

"Let's get something nice for tea," she said. "Look, they've got that cake with the piggy face on it – you like that one, don't you?"

"Like that one!" said Ruby.

"I'll just pop it into the trolley," said Mum.

Ruby watched the cake go in and twisted around to look at it.

"*HOLD* the piggy cake?" she asked.

"No, no!" said Mum. "Leave it in the trolley. OK? Just leave it."

"Just leave it," agreed Ruby, nodding wisely.

"That's right," said Mum, nervously. "Just *LEAVE* it – OK?"

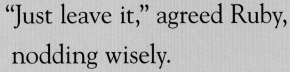

"Just *HOLD* it?" Ruby asked again, smiling very sweetly. "Just *HOLD* the piggy cake."

THEN MUM MADE A BIG MISTAKE.

"All right then," she said, taking the box out of the trolley. "Just *HOLD* it, OK?"

Ruby held out her arms
and wiggled her fingers.

"Just *HOLD* it," she agreed,
grabbing the box and
clutching it tightly.

"That's right," said Mum,
"just *HOLD* it – OK?"

Ruby clutched the cake a bit *too* tightly. Then she looked up at her mum and smiled – a very *determined* smile.

"HAVE the piggy cake!" said Ruby, very loudly. "HAVE the piggy cake NOW!!"
Ruby squeezed the box and the cake fell out.

"No, NO!" said Mum, trying to grab the cake. "Give the cake to Mummy!"

"HAVE THE PIGGY CAKE!" yelled Ruby. "HAVE THE PIGGY CAKE NOW!"

Mum tried to lift Ruby out of the seat, but she stuck her legs out straight and fell over backwards.

Mum tried to grab the cake but Ruby held on to it. EVERYONE WAS LOOKING!

Finally, Mum wrestled the squashed cake from Ruby's clutches and put what was left of it back into the trolley.

Ruby was screaming her head off. "GIVE ME THE PIGGY CAKE! HAVE THE PIGGY CAKE! AAAAAAAH! WANT IT NOW!"

Ruby carried on screaming while Mum paid for the shopping.

"I'm so sorry about this," said Mum to the check-out lady. "I think she must be tired. You're not *usually* like this, are you, Ruby?"

But Ruby was plunging head first into the back of the trolley.
"GIVE ME THE PIGGY CAKE NOW!!!" she screamed. "AAAAAAH!!!"

Mum packed the bags as fast as possible, crammed Ruby
into the pushchair and hurried out of the shop.

EVERYONE WAS STILL LOOKING.

Ruby went on yelling all the way home.
"GIVE ME THE PIGGY CAKE! AAAAAH!! AAAAAH!!!
WANT IT NOW!!!! AAAAAAAH!!!!!"

"RUBY!" said Mum. "For goodness' sake! Everyone's looking at you – stop that noise at once."

But Ruby didn't stop at once
– in fact, she didn't stop at all
until they got to the front door.

Mum pushed the pushchair into the hall and sat down
at the bottom of the stairs.
Ruby was very tired and Mum was very cross.

"Now then, Ruby," said Mum, sternly.
"You were very naughty."

"*Very* naughty," agreed
Ruby, sadly.

"So, what do you say
to Mummy?" asked Mum.

Ruby smiled her best, sorriest smile and said in a teeny, tiny voice,

"Have the piggy cake ...

please?"